DINK, JOSH, AND RUTH ROSE
AREN'T THE ONLY KID DETECTIVES!

WHAT ABOUT
YOU

CAN YOU FIND THE HIDDEN MESSAGE
INSIDE THIS BOOK?

There are 26 illustrations in this book,
not counting the one on the title page,
the map at the beginning, or the picture
of the missing necklace that repeats at
the start of many of the chapters. In
each of the 26 illustrations, there's a
hidden letter. If you can find all the
letters, you will spell out a secret
message!

If you're stumped, the answer is on
the bottom of page 117.

HAPPY DETECTING!

*This book is dedicated to my nephews
Bob and Bobby, and my niece, Desiree.*
—R.R.

To Academy School reader Max Cobb
—J.S.G.

Text copyright © 2007 by Ron Roy
Cover art copyright © 2015 by Stephen Gilpin
Interior illustrations copyright © 2007 by John Steven Gurney

All rights reserved. Published in the United States by Random House Children's Books, a division of Random House LLC, a Penguin Random House Company, New York. Originally published in paperback by Random House Children's Books, New York, in 2007.

Random House and the colophon and A to Z Mysteries are registered trademarks and A Stepping Stone Book and the colophon and the A to Z Mysteries colophon are trademarks of Random House LLC.

Visit us on the Web!
SteppingStonesBooks.com
randomhousekids.com

Educators and librarians, for a variety of teaching tools, visit us at RHTeachersLibrarians.com

Library of Congress Cataloging-in-Publication Data
Roy, Ron.
Mayflower treasure hunt / by Ron Roy ; illustrated by John Steven Gurney.
p. cm. — (A to Z mysteries. Super edition ; #2) "A Stepping Stone Book."
Summary: When Dink, Josh, and Ruth Rose visit Plymouth, Massachusetts, for Thanksgiving, they uncover a mystery that dates back to the landing of the Pilgrims.
ISBN 978-0-375-83937-5 (trade) — ISBN 978-0-375-93937-2 (lib. bdg.) —
ISBN 978-0-307-49673-7 (ebook)
[1. Mayflower (ship)—Fiction. 2. Buried treasure—Fiction. 3. Mystery and detective stories. 4. Plymouth (Mass.)—History—17th century—Fiction.] I. Gurney, John Steven, ill. II. Title. III. Series: Roy, Ron. A to Z mysteries Super edition ; #2.
PZ7.R8139 May 2007 [Fic]—dc22 2006015992

Printed in the United States of America
24 23 22 21 20

This book has been officially leveled by using the F&P Text Level Gradient™ Leveling System.

Random House Children's Books supports the First Amendment and celebrates the right to read.

A to Z Mysteries

SUPER EDITION 2

Mayflower Treasure Hunt

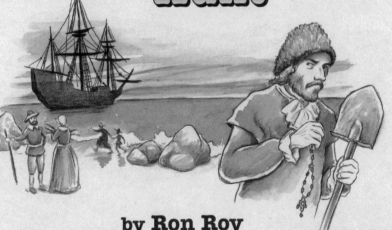

by Ron Roy

illustrated by
John Steven Gurney

WITHDRAWN

A STEPPING STONE BOOK™

Random House 🏠 New York

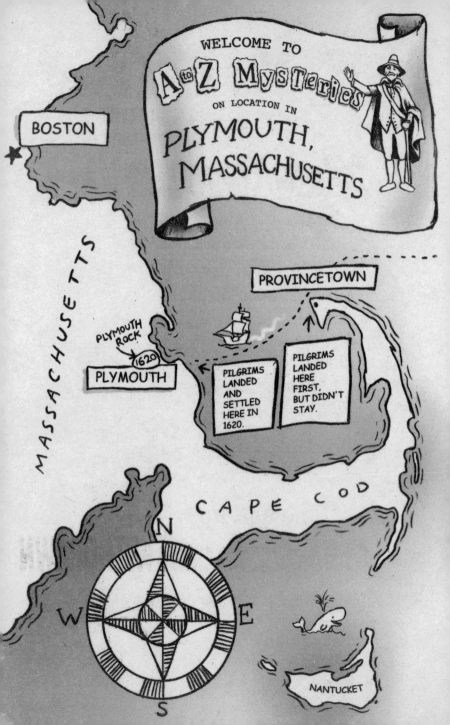

THE MAYFLOWER II

FORECASTLE

CONTAINS THE GALLEY, ALSO KNOWN AS THE KITCHEN.

THE CREW'S QUARTERS

'TWEEN DECKS

THIS IS WHERE THE 102 PILGRIMS LIVED AND SLEPT.

THE TOTAL SPACE WAS 80 FEET LONG, 24 FEET WIDE, AND 5½ FEET HIGH.

THE HOLD

THE BOTTOM LEVEL OF THE SHIP, USED FOR STORAGE.

CHAPTER 1

Josh peered inside the deep, dark oven. "Wow!" he said, backing away. "It smells like bacon in there!"

A tall man standing next to Josh laughed. "Aye, son, we roasted a pig for the tourists this past Sunday." The man wore baggy pants, a navy blue shirt with a white ruffled collar, and boots. He had dark curly hair and a thick beard.

Dink, Josh, and Ruth Rose were inside the cook room on board the *Mayflower II*, in Plymouth, Massachusetts. This ship was a replica of the original *Mayflower*, which brought English passengers to Massachusetts in 1620.

The kids' families had decided to have this year's Thanksgiving meal here, in the town where the first *Mayflower* passengers had landed. Dink's mother had driven the three kids to the historic town. Everyone else would arrive tomorrow, the day before Thanksgiving.

Dink's mother was spending the day with an old college friend who lived a few miles away. So the kids were on their own until she got back at five o'clock.

Ruth Rose had bought a guidebook. Inside were pictures and information about the *Mayflower* and other sites in Plymouth. She turned to a page that showed an inside view of the *Mayflower*. "Is this where the *Mayflower* passengers did all the cooking?" she asked.

"Aye, most of the meals were prepared here in the galley by the boat's cook, lassie," the man said. "But a few of the women brought their own small iron stoves. They lit them on deck to cook stew or soup or porridge for their children."

A few other tourists were exploring the boat. Workers, dressed the way the Pilgrims had dressed, were stationed around the decks to explain things to the visitors. In fact, the workers were all actors pretending they had just arrived aboard the real *Mayflower*. They could even speak the way the original passengers spoke.

Dink looked around the small, dark galley, or kitchen. He was amazed that food for over a hundred people was cooked in this tiny, cramped space! Of course there was no refrigerator or stove. Just this dark oven made of bricks, a small worktable, and a couple of crude benches.

It was a mild week in late November. Dink, Josh, and Ruth Rose wore sweatshirts and jeans. Ruth Rose's outfit was all blue. She liked to wear clothes that matched. Even her headband matched her sneakers!

"Where did the passengers sleep?" Dink asked.

The man pointed down a narrow set of stairs. "'Tween decks, down those stairs," the man said. "Careful as you go!"

The kids walked down the stairs, holding on to a rope that had been attached to one wall. A woman in a long purple dress stood at the bottom. She wore a tight white hat that covered her hair. She smiled at the kids.

"Yes, this is where we slept and lived for nearly ten weeks—and crowded it was!" she said.

The room was narrow and dark.

There were a few small openings high on the walls for light and fresh air. A mattress lay in one corner, and a couple of wood sleeping platforms had been attached to one of the walls. The kids checked out a row of hammocks that were strung up along one side of the space.

"Didn't everyone get a mattress?" asked Josh.

The woman shook her head. "No. A few of us had mattresses stuffed with straw," she said. "Some slept right on the wood floor. I slept in a hammock."

"It *must* have been crowded," Ruth Rose said. "I read that there were over a hundred passengers!"

"Yes, and about thirty crew," the woman said. "'Tween decks here 'twas crowded and smelly. The rats would come around looking for food. We'd feel them at night walking over our beds.

Many of us got sick, and one passenger died."

Dink noticed clay pots under some of the hammocks. He knew from his reading that these were called chamber pots. There were no bathrooms on the *Mayflower*.

"Did you bring furniture and stuff with you?" Dink asked. He was trying to imagine what it would be like to live in this dark room for more than two months!

"Aye, some did, but it was kept down below in the hold," the woman said. She pointed to a wide opening cut into the wood deck. The dark hole was covered by a grate. It looked like the grates that cover street sewers, only bigger. Dink peered down through the grate slats. He could see a large pile of straw-filled mattresses.

"Everything we brought was kept

there—clothing, furniture, keepsakes," the woman went on. "We were not allowed to touch our things during the crossing."

"Why not?" asked Ruth Rose. "What if you needed more clothing?"

"Thievery is why not," the woman said, shaking her head. "The boat master was afraid we'd steal each other's things, so the hold was off-limits.

"Still and all, items were stolen. My friend Emma Browne had her jewelry taken. She had packed it with her belongings down there. When we reached land and were allowed to see our possessions, dear Emma's necklace was gone. Emma cried for a week. She said it had belonged to her grandmother."

"Did they ever find out who took it?" Josh asked.

The woman shook her head. "No,

but we all think it was that Lawrence Mudgett, a crew member," she said. "He was in jail in England before the crossing. Oh, he was a mean 'un. Mudgett used to kick the dogs and the children if they got in his way. All the passengers hated and feared him. Aye, Mudgett is the *Mayflower* thief!"

"There were dogs on the *Mayflower*?" Josh asked.

"Aye, two, and a few cats. They helped by eating the mice and rats," the woman said. "Other animals came across with us. Chickens and geese for eggs, and pigs and goats for their meat. We kept some alive so we'd have livestock once we landed."

More tourists were coming down the stairs, so Dink, Josh, and Ruth Rose explored the rest of the boat. They talked to more workers, all dressed in costume and speaking with British accents. As the kids were leaving the ship, they were stopped by a man wearing baggy black pants and a tight-fitting black jacket. His hat was black, too, showing off his ruffled white collar and white beard.

"Did you enjoy the tour?" the man asked. "I am the boat master, what you Americans call the ship's captain."

"This boat is awesome!" Josh said. "But I don't think I'd want to live on it like the Pilgrims did!"

"We were very thankful when we landed," the boat master said.

"We heard about a man named Mudgett," Dink said. "Did he really steal stuff from the passengers?"

The man nodded. "Yes, I'm afraid so," he said. "Poor Emma Browne lost her jewelry."

"What happened to the thief?" asked Ruth Rose.

The boat master looked over the side of the ship. "He disappeared, missy," he said. "When we landed, there was a terrible windstorm. We all stayed in our quarters to wait it out. The storm finally let up, but we never saw Mudgett again."

The boat master leaned down. "Some think he escaped with the jewelry, then made his way back to England," he said. "Myself, I believe he fell overboard and became a meal for sharks!"

CHAPTER 2

Josh looked over the side of the *Mayflower II*. "There are sharks here?" he said.

The boat master laughed. "I don't know about now," he said, "but I saw quite a few during the crossing. They followed the boat to eat the kitchen leavings that the crew tossed overboard."

"We want to see Plymouth Rock next," Ruth Rose said. "Can you tell us where it is?"

The man pointed to a small concrete building not far away from the boat. "'Tis under that roof," he said. "Be sure to visit the Pilgrim Hall Museum, too. 'Tis a short walk from the rock."

The kids left the *Mayflower II*, then hiked across a parking lot. They passed through a small grove of trees and came to a concrete building with columns in front. Behind the columns was a black fence. A few other people were standing by the fence, looking down at a large gray rock. The date 1620 had been etched into one side of it.

Dink, Josh, and Ruth Rose joined the people at the fence. Ruth Rose opened her guidebook to the right page. "No one knows for sure if the Pilgrims really stepped on this rock when they got off the *Mayflower*," she said. "But the ship landed near here, so they might have."

Suddenly Josh lifted his head in the air. He sniffed, turning his head into the breeze. "I smell food," he said. "I'm hungry."

Dink looked at his friend. "Again?"

"I'm a growing boy," Josh said. "If I don't eat eight times a day, my brain will shrink."

Ruth Rose and Dink burst out laughing.

"Well, let's go find food fast," Dink teased. "We don't want your brain to get any smaller!"

The kids chose a restaurant across the street from the Pilgrim Hall Museum.

They each ordered a tuna sandwich and hot chocolate. After they paid, Ruth Rose walked over to a game machine called the Iron Claw. It was filled with toy prizes.

"These things are rip-offs," Josh told Ruth Rose. He dropped some change into a candy machine, got peanut-filled M&M's, and shoved the bag into a pocket.

"Well, I want to get that stuffed mouse for my cat," Ruth Rose said.

Using the joystick, she moved the iron claw until it was inches above the mouse. She pulled the stick forward, lowering the claw. Then she pushed the button on the stick, and the claw grabbed at the mouse. But at the last second, the claw snagged a plastic necklace.

"Told you so!" Josh said.

The claw brought the prize to the

little opening in front of Ruth Rose. With a rattle, the necklace landed in the tray. She pulled it out.

The necklace had a cheap tin chain and ten plastic "diamonds" the size of grapes.

"Oooh, look at those huge diamonds!" Josh teased. "Gee, that necklace must be worth about . . . NOTHING!"

"It's not so bad," Dink said. "And it's probably worth more than the quarter it cost you."

"Well, I like it," Ruth Rose said. She slid the necklace over her head and tucked it beneath her sweatshirt.

The kids hurried across Court Street to the museum.

Inside, there were four little rooms. Each was filled with stuff from the *Mayflower* or from England in the 1600s. They saw furniture, cooking pots, and a hand-carved bench that came over on

the *Mayflower*. There were several paint-
ings showing the *Mayflower* and some of
its passengers.

Dink stopped in front of a glass dis-
play dome. Inside, he saw a quill pen
and ink holder. A small sign said that
these writing tools had belonged to
William Bradford, the governor of the
New Plymouth Colony. He later wrote a
book called *History of Plymouth Plantation.*

"Hey, guys, over here," Josh said. He
was looking at a list inside a frame.
"These are the names of all the people
who came over on the *Mayflower!*" he
whispered.

There were 102 names on the list,
written alphabetically. Next to the names
were the dates when the people had
died, many in the winter of 1620.

"Look, there's Emma Browne," Ruth
Rose said. "It was her jewelry that

was stolen from the hold."

Below the passenger list was a shorter list of *Mayflower* crew members.

Dink quickly found Lawrence Mudgett. Next to his name was a question mark and "November 1620." "This is the guy who stole it," Dink reminded Josh and Ruth Rose.

A man had walked up behind the kids. "They never found him or the jewelry," the man said.

The kids turned and looked at the man. He was dressed in khakis and a blue shirt. His black hair was cut short.

"My name's Clint," the man said. "I'm a docent, a fancy word for 'guide.' I'm really an actor, but I do this for extra money."

He opened a plastic container of mints, popped one in his mouth, and held the container toward the kids. "Want one? They're cinnamon-flavored."

"No, thank you," the kids said.

Dink introduced himself and Josh and Ruth Rose. "We're staying at the Governor Bradford Hotel," he said. "Our families are going to have dinner on Thanksgiving Day like the Pilgrims did."

"If you're interested in Lawrence Mudgett, I can show you something," the man said.

He led them to a stack of thin booklets piled on a table. The title of the booklets was *Mudgett and the Missing Jewels: A Muddlesome Mayflower Mystery*.

The kids each took one of the booklets.

Ruth Rose opened her guidebook. "This says the *Mayflower* landed in another place before they came here to Plymouth," she said.

"Right, that was up near Provincetown," Clint said. He popped another mint. "The crew spent about a month

there exploring. But they couldn't find freshwater, and winter was coming. So the *Mayflower* set sail again, and ended up here in Plymouth. Some people figure Mudgett hid the loot in Provincetown, where they first hit land." Clint shook his head. "Can you imagine what those jewels would be worth today?"

Dink was looking at a little frame. Inside the frame was a charcoal drawing on a piece of cloth. It looked like a child's drawing of the *Mayflower* anchored near a shore. There was a beach with trees and big rocks. One rock was tall and very narrow with a pointy top. It leaned to one side and looked like it was ready to fall over. The rock resembled an eagle with its beak pointing up at the sky. The picture also showed a small boat on the shore, carrying about ten passengers.

"What's this?" Josh asked, looking

over Dink's shoulder at the picture.

"I think it's supposed to be the *Mayflower* landing," Ruth Rose said.

"Yeah, but where?" Dink asked. "I mean, is this the first landing, or is it when they got here to Plymouth?"

"They think it's up the coast in Provincetown," Clint said. "See those tall rocks? Some of them are still there."

The docent pointed to a small sign on the wall next to the drawing. "Excuse me, I have more customers," Clint said as he walked away.

Dink read the words out loud: "This drawing was found in the belongings of Mr. Lawrence Mudgett, who disappeared. It is believed that he drew the picture in November 1620, on the occasion of the first landfall."

"Gosh, if Mudgett drew this," Josh said, "maybe it's a map of where he hid the jewels!"

CHAPTER 3

Dink examined the drawing. "It doesn't look like a map to me," he said. "There are no directions or measurements, and nothing that says 'X marks the spot.'"

"Plus, it's all smudgy," Ruth Rose said. "This looks like a drawing done by some little kid, not a grown man. Why would Mudgett even keep it?"

"He'd keep it if it was a map telling where he hid the jewelry," Josh said. "Maybe the guy couldn't draw very well. Maybe he made it smudgy on purpose, so if anyone saw it, they wouldn't know what it was supposed to be."

Josh walked over and asked the woman at the door if she had a magnifying glass he could borrow. She found one, and Josh brought it back. He held it up to the drawing.

Ruth Rose giggled. "Josh is looking for a little sign that says 'Jewels buried here!'"

"Very funny," Josh said. "I just think it's weird that the guy everyone says took the jewelry also had this picture."

"But we don't know if he even hid the necklace anywhere," Ruth Rose said. "Maybe he had it with him when he disappeared. Maybe the jewels are inside some shark's belly!"

"Right," Dink said. "He could've kept the jewelry on him." He looked at Josh. "Okay, I guess it does seem strange that Mudgett had this picture if it wasn't important. But if Clint is right, this drawing shows where the *Mayflower* first landed, up on Cape Cod. If Mudgett really hid the jewelry there, how would he get back there once the boat reached Plymouth?"

The three kids stood there staring at the childish drawing.

"What if Mudgett stole the jewels, then when the *Mayflower* got to land, he

went ashore in one of those explorer boats?" Josh suggested, thinking out loud. "He hid what he stole. Then back on the *Mayflower* that night, he drew this picture to remind himself where he'd hidden it. He planned to go back for the jewels after the boat had been thoroughly searched. But before he had a chance, the *Mayflower* sailed again and landed here. And then Mudgett drowned during a storm."

"Or got gobbled up by a shark," Ruth Rose added.

"I suppose it could have happened that way," Dink said. "So if you're right—"

"If I'm right, the jewels are still wherever he hid them!" Josh finished for him. "He never got back there, and the jewels have been waiting for someone to find them since 1620!"

"But where?" Ruth Rose asked.

"Wherever this piece of shoreline is," Josh said, pointing to the drawing. "Who's got something to write with?"

Ruth Rose handed Josh a pencil and a sheet of paper. Josh began making his own sketch of the drawing.

"Wait a second," Ruth Rose said as she watched Josh's sketch take shape. "What's that where the eagle's beak should be?" She pointed to the rock that looked like an eagle. "Doesn't the eagle's mouth look like an *X*?"

Josh moved the magnifying glass back over the drawing hanging on the wall. He focused it on the top part of the pointy rock. Up close, it did resemble an eagle's head. And the eagle's beak did look a bit like an *X*.

"It looks like the eagle is carrying a couple of branches to its nest," Dink said, squinting one eye.

Josh put his face practically on the

framed drawing. "It does sort of look like an *X*," Josh said. "I wish this wasn't so smudged."

Clint had walked back to them. "If you want to go see the place where the *Mayflower* first landed, there's a ferry-boat called the *Sea Witch*," he said. "It leaves from the pier next to the *Mayflower II*."

Josh folded his sketch and slid it into his pocket.

"How long does it take to get there?" Ruth Rose asked.

"Under an hour," Clint said. He glanced at his watch. "The next one leaves at one o'clock."

Dink checked his own watch. "My mom expects us at the hotel by five," he told Clint. "Could we make it back here by then?"

"Oh sure," the friendly docent said. "Plenty of time."

The kids thanked Clint, then hurried back toward the pier. They had no trouble finding the ferry called the *Sea Witch*. There was a colorful sign on the dock showing a life-size drawing of a Halloween witch riding her broom over the ocean. Beneath the picture were the words SEA WITCH TO PROVINCETOWN.

Dink glanced farther along the dock where the ferry was moored. The *Sea Witch* was twice as long as the *Mayflower II*, and the decks were crowded with people.

Suddenly a loud horn blast came from the ferry. "That must be a warning to hurry up," Dink said, looking at his watch. "We still have ten minutes."

They bought tickets at a small booth, then walked up a gangway to an outer deck. They stood at the rail, looking down at the *Mayflower II*, which was moored on the other side of the pier.

"Let's go inside," Josh suggested.

The kids walked to the seating cabin and sat on a bench. Other passengers sat nearby. There were tall windows on all sides, providing excellent views of the sky and water.

Another horn went off.

"Five minutes," Dink announced.

An old woman entered the cabin and looked around for a seat. She wore sunglasses, and a shawl over her thick gray hair. Her long black coat reached to her shoes. The woman shuffled over to a bench in a far corner of the cabin.

They all heard a final horn blast. The engine started, and the deck under their feet began to hum and shudder. Soon the *Sea Witch* was backing away from its mooring.

"We're leaving!" Ruth Rose said. She got up and hurried outside to stand at the railing. Josh went with her.

Several of the passengers moved to inside windows. The *Sea Witch* had left the pier and was cruising past the shoreline. Outside the windows, seagulls shrieked as they soared alongside. Some kids were throwing potato chips into the air, hoping the gulls would grab them.

Dink noticed that the old woman was watching him. Or was she? Her eyes were covered by the sunglasses, so maybe he was mistaken. But he had a feeling that she was looking at him.

Dink stood up and walked a few yards away. He casually walked back, sneaking a quick look at the woman. Now her head was down, and she seemed to be sleeping.

As Dink watched the drowsing woman, he realized that there was something familiar about her. Had he seen that mole on her face before, or

those gloves with the fingers cut off?

No, he hadn't met her before, but there was still something about her that . . . then he laughed at himself.

This woman looked like the cartoon witch he'd noticed on the dock sign. The cartoon witch wore a scraggly dress and a long scarf and had a mole on her face, just like the woman sitting opposite Dink.

Dink shook his head, feeling foolish. Then he walked outside to find Josh and Ruth Rose. A gust of wind made Dink shiver, and he felt goose bumps march up his arms.

CHAPTER 4

Dink found Josh and Ruth Rose standing at the railing. Below them, the sea rolled beneath the boat. Seaweed clumps drifted by, and one passenger pointed at some jumping fish. The sun glistened off their silvery scales.

"Josh wouldn't share his M&M's with the seagulls," Ruth Rose teased.

Dink laughed and took a deep breath of the cold air. It smelled of salt and something sweet. Soon land came into view, and the ferry began to slow.

"Won't it be awesome if we find those stolen jewels?" Josh asked.

"What's really awesome is that the *Mayflower* sailed right where we are almost four hundred years ago," Ruth Rose said. "Think how happy those people must have been to see land!"

Straight ahead, the kids could see trees and buildings come into view. Then red and green buoys appeared. The ferry kept to the left of the red buoys all the way to the long pier.

Passengers began walking toward the stairs that would take them off the boat. As the kids followed, Dink kept his eyes open for the old woman with the mole on her face. He didn't spot her, but he wasn't surprised. There were dozens of other people in the line leaving the boat.

Once they were on solid ground again, Dink, Josh, and Ruth Rose walked along the pier. They started following a small sign that pointed toward the center of Provincetown.

"Wait a minute, guys," Ruth Rose said. She was pulling her guidebook from the pouch in her sweatshirt. She read for a minute. "Okay, this says there's a place called First Encounter Beach. It's where the Pilgrims first landed and where they first saw Indians."

"So where is this beach?" Josh asked.

Ruth Rose turned her guidebook so Dink and Josh could see the map. "I think we take a right off the pier," she said. "See? That doesn't look too far."

Ruth Rose was right. Five minutes of fast walking brought them to a wind-swept beach. A plaque on a boulder said FIRST ENCOUNTER BEACH.

"The *Mayflower* wouldn't have been able to land here," Dink said, remembering what he'd read in school. "They anchored pretty far out and used

smaller boats to get to land."

Josh unfolded the sketch he'd made in the Pilgrim Hall Museum. The shoreline in that drawing looked nothing like the one stretching in front of them. "So where do we start?" he asked.

Ruth Rose looked at Josh's drawing. "Trees and shorelines could change a lot in four hundred years," she said. "But that tall rock might still be here somewhere."

"I don't see any rocks," Dink said, "let alone one that looks like an eagle."

The three kids turned in a circle, trying to spot a tall, pointy rock. They saw a few trees that looked really old and some beach cottages. One man was scraping the bottom of a rowboat in his yard.

"Let's ask him," Ruth Rose suggested.

The kids walked over and told the

man what they were looking for. He glanced at Josh's sketch. "Nope. Nothin' like that around here," he said. "I been here thirty years and never seen a rock like that."

Dink had an idea. "Do you know where the Pilgrims came ashore?" he

asked. "Was it really here, on this beach?"

The man pointed a hundred yards to the left. "The Provincetown Historical Society says they landed over there, where that small grove of pine trees grows right up to the water's edge," he said.

They thanked the man and hiked toward the pine trees. The spot was silent except for the whisper of a breeze blowing through pine needles. A few seagulls floated overhead. Dink felt strange, realizing he might be standing where Pilgrims had once walked!

"Okay, if you're that Mudgett guy and you land here, what do you do next?" Josh asked.

"He wouldn't be alone," Ruth Rose said, reading from her guidebook. "There'd be other crew members in the boat and some passengers. It says kids came ashore to get exercise, and women came to wash clothes."

"Mudgett would want to find a private place to hide the jewels," Dink added. "Somehow he must have found the rock we saw in the picture."

"But there is no rock," Josh said, looking disappointed.

"Maybe it's underwater now," Ruth Rose said. "Maybe the beach that was here got covered up!"

"Oh great," Josh said. "We have to find a rock under the ocean?"

"I've never read anything that says the beach where they landed is underwater now," Dink said.

"I haven't, either," Ruth Rose said. "If Mudgett really had the jewels with him, he'd want to go as far away from other people as he could. So maybe he found the rock further away from the shore."

"But the drawing shows the rock near the beach," Josh said, pointing to his own sketch.

"There are some more cottages on the other side of that little bridge," Ruth Rose said. "Maybe someone knows about the rock."

The kids trekked over the bridge and walked up to the first house they came to. A woman opened the door. "Yes?" she said.

Josh showed her his sketch. "We're trying to find this rock," he said.

The woman took a close look at the sketch. Then she shook her head. "I don't remember ever seeing anything like this," she said. "Sorry, kids."

The door swung shut, and the kids started to walk away.

"Hey, I just thought of something," the woman said, opening the door again. She pointed toward a tall, bare tree. "There's a little park there. It's called Rock Park. There are a few big boulders, but nothing tall and pointy like the one you showed me. Anyway, good luck!"

The kids hurried toward the tall tree. Beneath it, they found a couple of benches and a set of swings. There was a sandy place near a row of flat rocks partly buried in the sand. Dink saw a plastic pail and a little shovel under one of the benches. The whole area was

surrounded by boulders as tall as Ruth Rose.

"Well, unless the rock shrank over the years, it isn't here," Josh said.

Dink noticed something shiny on one of the boulders. He walked over to see what it was. "Hey, guys, check this out," he said, kneeling to read a brass plate.

WELCOME TO ROCK PARK. IT IS BELIEVED THAT SOME OF THE *MAYFLOWER* PASSENGERS PASSED THROUGH HERE AS THEY EXPLORED THIS AREA OF PROVINCETOWN IN

NOVEMBER 1620. THERE WERE MORE
BOULDERS THEN. THE ROW OF FIVE
FLAT ROCKS BEHIND YOU WAS ONCE A
SINGLE MONOLITH THAT STOOD
TWENTY FEET TALL. YEARS AGO, THE
ROCK TOPPLED AND BROKE INTO
SECTIONS DURING A HURRICANE.

Dink, Josh, and Ruth Rose whipped
around to look at the flat rocks that had
once been a tall rock. A few people were
walking near the park. Dink wondered
if they had come on the ferry.

Dink noticed someone sitting on one
of the benches. She was hunched over,

with a long shawl covering her head and most of her face. It was the same old woman he had seen on the ferry.

"You see that woman?" Dink whispered to Josh and Ruth Rose.

"What about her?" Josh said.

"I think she's following us!" Dink said. "She was watching me on the ferry, too."

"Maybe she's just following the trail of the Pilgrims, like we are," Ruth Rose said. "She looks like she's sleeping."

"How did she get here so fast?" Dink said, keeping his voice low. "One minute that bench was empty, and then she appeared out of nowhere!"

"Dink, a lot of the people on the ferry were probably coming here," Ruth Rose said. "Maybe that woman wanted to see the place where the Pilgrims landed."

"Yeah, I guess you're right," Dink said.

"You know, if this was a tall rock

before it fell over, one of these five pieces must have been the pointy top," Josh said. "Like in my drawing."

The kids looked at the five flat rocks. They were all in a row. A few inches of each rock was exposed above the sand.

"If the rock fell over straight, the top part should be one of the two end ones," Ruth Rose said. "Maybe there was a hole in the top of the rock, and that's why Mudgett hid the jewels there."

"You're right, Ruth Rose," Josh said. "So let's dig around the two end pieces first." He dropped to his knees and started scraping sand away from the flat rocks. Dink and Ruth Rose joined him.

Dink grabbed the plastic pail and shovel. The old woman was still on the bench. Her chin was on her chest, and she was snoring quietly.

Dink handed the shovel to Ruth Rose and the pail to Josh. "I'll try to find something else to dig with," he said. He walked toward the tall tree and found a dead branch. One end was sharp and flat, perfect for scooping sand.

Josh was examining his sketch again. "Which of these two end rocks seems to have a pointy end?" he asked. "That should be the top, the eagle's mouth."

"I can't tell yet," Ruth Rose said. She was twenty feet away from Josh, tossing sand out of a hole she'd dug at the very end of the rock.

The kids dug as the afternoon grew colder and the sun disappeared behind some clouds. Dink checked his watch. "We have to be on the four o'clock ferry no matter what," he said. "It's three-fifteen now."

They dug faster and faster. Piles of sand grew around their knees. They uncovered all sorts of things that had gotten left behind over the years: empty bottles, a button, part of a comic book.

"Guys, my rock is getting narrow! I think it has a pointy end!" Ruth Rose said. The boys scrambled over to where she was digging. Ruth Rose had exposed about two feet more of the rock. They all helped her dig until the entire end was visible.

It did taper to a kind of point. But they couldn't find a hole where anyone might have hidden something. It was impossible to tell if this part of the rock was the same as the eagle's mouth in Josh's sketch. Or if this had been at the very top of the rock when it was still standing.

Dink felt disappointed. He'd begun to get excited about solving this 400-year-old mystery. Maybe someone else had found the stolen jewels years ago. Heck, some squirrel could have carried them off!

"Let's dig this whole area up," he said. "There might be another section of rock that's buried."

Their two-foot hole became three feet deep and three feet wide. Dink's fingers were sore, and one of his knuckles was bleeding.

"Yuck!" Josh yelled suddenly, falling back on his knees. "I found a dead animal!"

Dink looked at what had made Josh's face turn white. It was about the size of a hamster and covered with rotted brown skin.

Dink used his stick to lift the thing out of the hole. The brown skin fell apart.

"OH MY GOSH!" Ruth Rose yelled.

It wasn't an animal skin at all. It was a decayed leather bag. As it fell away, something still hung from Dink's stick.

It was a necklace.

CHAPTER 5

"The *Mayflower* jewels!" Dink said.

Tiny roots clung to it. Still, the metal looked like gold, and held at least fifteen blue gemstones.

"We were right!" Josh said. "Mudgett hid the loot here, then drew that picture as a map!"

Dink pulled his stick over and dropped the necklace into Ruth Rose's hands. "I'll keep it in my sweatshirt pouch," she said. She gathered up the remnants of the leather bag and put that inside with the necklace.

Just then the kids heard a long, loud

horn blast in the distance.

"It's the ferry!" Dink said. He checked his watch. "Quarter to four. Let's go!"

The three kids took off running. As Dink passed the bench where the woman had been dozing, he noticed that she was gone. *How does she keep disappearing?* he wondered as they raced across the beach toward the ferry landing.

With only a minute to spare, they tore up the walkway to the *Sea Witch*'s outer deck. Out of breath, they stepped into the cabin and huddled on a bench.

"Still got it?" Dink whispered to Ruth Rose.

She nodded and patted the lump in her sweatshirt pouch.

The final horn blast sounded, and the kids sat back. Dink closed his eyes. The boat's engine came to life and they slowly began to move. Dink grinned. He couldn't wait to tell his mom about their adventure.

"She's baaaack," Josh whispered in Dink's ear.

Dink opened his eyes as Josh nudged him.

The old woman had taken a seat not far from where the kids sat.

Dink stared at her. *Don't get paranoid,* he told himself. *She could be just another tourist. Maybe she just wanted to see the place where the* Mayflower *first landed. She's probably some nice old schoolteacher trying to learn more about the Pilgrims. Or maybe she's a writer, doing research for a book. She's not a witch who disappears, and she's not following us!*

Dink relaxed. He watched through the windows as two kids and their parents tried to persuade seagulls to snatch food from their fingers.

"What should we do with the . . . you-know-what?" Ruth Rose asked.

"Sell it and get rich," Josh said.

"Sell it to who?" Dink asked. "Who'd buy it?"

"We're not selling anything," Ruth Rose said. "That . . . package belongs to that poor woman who lost it."

"She's dead," Josh said.

"She might have relatives," Dink said. "Her heirs should get it."

Josh giggled. "Maybe I'm her heir," he said.

As the kids talked, Dink glanced over toward the old woman. At least she wasn't staring at Dink this time. She was gazing out the windows. As Dink watched, she took something from a pocket and slipped it into her mouth, then sat back and closed her eyes.

The sky was growing darker. Black

clouds had blocked the sun, and even inside the cabin Dink felt cold. He shivered, shut his eyes, and huddled deeper into his sweatshirt. The boat's gentle movement made him sleepy.

"Wake up," Josh said, giving Dink a nudge. "We're almost at the pier."

Dink opened his eyes and blinked. He had been asleep. Everyone was inside the cabin now. A wind had come up, and it had grown dark. Thick snowflakes were slapping against the glass. An early moon came and went behind black clouds. Lights in the cabin ceiling blinked on.

"It's twenty after five," Ruth Rose said. "Will your mom be upset that we're late?"

"Probably," Dink said. "But she'll forgive us when we show her the you-know-what!"

The ferry began to ease into its

mooring place alongside the pier. The kids got in the long line of passengers snaking its way toward the exits. The old woman was a few people ahead of Dink in the line. She had wrapped her shawl over her head and shoulders. Dink wondered how far she had to walk in the blowing snow.

Ten minutes later, the kids were hurrying toward the Governor Bradford Hotel. The moon seemed to move with them. It was almost completely dark and still snowing. Dink could see their footprints on the now-white sidewalk.

"There it is!" Dink said as the hotel came into sight.

The kids brushed the snow off their shoulders and stamped their feet outside the lobby door. Dink pushed it open, half expecting to see his mother standing there with an annoyed look on her face.

A woman was at the counter. Her back was to the kids, but Dink knew this wasn't his mother with the shawl, the matted gray hair, the ankle-length dress. It was the old woman from the boat, and she was talking to the clerk.

The clerk looked up and nodded toward the kids.

Dink felt his throat close up. Panicked, he spun around, grabbing for Josh and Ruth Rose. He yanked them back through the door into the snow.

"What's going on?" Josh asked.

"It's her!" Dink hissed. "That old woman has been everywhere we go, and now she's in our hotel!"

"Dinkus, it's not *our* hotel," Josh said. "She could be staying here, just like us."

"But I keep seeing her!" Dink insisted, watching through the window. The woman was hurrying toward the door.

"She's coming outside!" Dink cried. "Let's get out of here!"

The kids raced away from the hotel entrance. Dink pulled Josh and Ruth Rose behind a row of hedges near the street. The old woman was standing in front of the hotel. She was looking around, one hand shielding her eyes.

"She's looking for us," Dink whispered. "I was right—she's after us!"

"But who *is* she?" Ruth Rose asked.

Josh giggled. "She's Emma Browne's ghost," he whispered. "She knows you have her jewels!"

As they watched, the woman took a few steps toward them. She glanced down at the ground, then looked directly at the hedges.

"She saw the footprints!" Dink hissed. "She knows we're here! Come on!"

With Dink in the lead, the kids took

off across the street. They hid behind a Dumpster and watched the hotel. The old woman was standing near the hedges now, bent over.

"Dink, we're gonna freeze out here," Josh said. "Our parents will find us on Thanksgiving, three ice sculptures!"

"Josh is right," Ruth Rose said. "We can't just stand out here all night."

Dink blew snowflakes out of his eyes. "All she has to do is follow our footprints," he said. "We have to hide until she gives up."

"We could go back to the boat," Ruth Rose said.

"The ferry?" Dink said. He spit snow out of his mouth.

"No, the *Mayflower*," Ruth Rose said over the wind. "She won't bother us with a crowd of people around."

"It's worth a try," Dink said. He looked up at all the falling snowflakes.

"Maybe the new snow will cover our tracks."

It took them only a few minutes to reach the *Mayflower II*. It sat in the harbor, rocking on small waves as the wind blew snowflakes around its dark shape. Over the wind, Dink could hear the sail ropes thunking against the tall wooden masts.

Dink found a trash can and lifted the lid. He pulled out a newspaper and handed Josh and Ruth Rose each a section.

"Let's use these to wipe away our footprints," he said.

The kids walked backward, brushing their footprints with the papers. When they got to the boat, they stuffed the newspapers inside their sweatshirts.

They ran up the gangway toward the fence and gate that let visitors onto the boat.

"The gate is locked," Ruth Rose said.

"The *Mayflower* is closed."

Dink turned and peered back the way they'd come. In his mind, he saw the old woman following their footprints. Would the snow cover them? Would she be fooled by their attempt to wipe their tracks away?

"Guys, I might have messed up," Dink admitted. "If we'd stayed at the hotel, that woman couldn't have done anything to us. Not with the clerk there. We could've just run up to our rooms."

"It's too late to worry about that now," Ruth Rose said. "Besides, it was my idea to come to the *Mayflower*. I didn't know it would be closed." She peered through the locked gate. "Let's climb over the fence. If we can hide on the *Mayflower*, she'll never find us."

"She's right," Josh said. He put his arm around Dink's shoulder. "We can pretend we're the Pilgrims during their first snowstorm in America!"

Ruth Rose began climbing. The boys found toeholds and followed her.

Once they were inside the fence, they ran aboard the *Mayflower II*. The ship looked ghostly under a covering of snow. The wind blew snow into their faces and froze their eyelashes.

"We have to get out of this snow," Josh said. He blew into his hands.

"Okay, let's go downstairs," Dink suggested. He led them past the dark galley. Now that they were out of the wind and snow, they felt warmer.

They climbed down the stairs to the deck where the Pilgrims had lived and slept. It was completely dark, only the moon's dim glow making its way into the space. Dink stopped over the grate that led down to the hold.

"This is creepy," Josh whispered. His voice shook, either from cold or fear.

Dink peered down through the grate into the darkness. "It'll be warmer down there," he said, pointing.

Suddenly they heard a thump on the deck above them. They jumped, bumping into each other. Josh fell over a pile of something and sprawled onto the floor.

"It's her! Help me move the grate!" Dink whispered.

The three kids tugged the wooden grate about fifteen inches. "A few more inches and we can fit!" Dink said.

"How do we get down there?" Ruth Rose asked. "It's deep!"

"There are some mattresses right below us," Dink said. "I remember them!"

"Are you sure?" Josh asked.

"No," Dink said.

And he jumped.

CHAPTER 6

Dink landed on the straw mattresses and fell backward onto the wooden deck. He knew he was on the very bottom of the boat. The wood felt cold and slimy under his fingers. He tried not to think about what he was touching. He moved out of the way and looked up. "Come on, it's okay!" he whispered.

Ruth Rose jumped next, and Dink helped steady her landing.

"Come on, Josh!" she said.

Dink could see Josh's silhouette against the moonlight behind him. Suddenly his head vanished.

Dink froze. Could the old woman have grabbed him?

"Josh!" Dink gasped.

And then Josh was falling through the air. He landed with a *whump* on the top mattress.

"I think she's on the boat!" Josh whispered. "I heard footsteps!"

The kids grabbed a couple of mattresses and dragged them into a far corner.

"She must be looking for us!" Dink said.

"If she notices the open grate, she'll know we're down here!" Ruth Rose said.

They sat and stared at the open space in the deck above them.

Dink could barely breathe. "She must know what we found, and she wants it," he said, keeping his voice to a whisper.

"How would she know?" Josh asked.

"She might have seen us dig it up," Ruth Rose said.

Dink remembered his surprise at seeing the old woman on the bench while they'd been digging.

Suddenly Ruth Rose gasped. She

pointed at the rim of the opening over their heads. A dark shape was moving slowly around the edge.

Dink thought it was the woman, but the shape was too small to be her head.

"It's a rat!" Josh choked out.

"What does it want?" asked Ruth Rose, wriggling closer to the boys.

Josh dug the M&M's bag out of his pocket. He stood up and walked beneath the opening. Using his best pitch, he threw the candy up and out of the hold. The rat disappeared.

"Aren't you glad I didn't feed those to the seagulls?" Josh asked Ruth Rose.

"You're my hero," she said.

The kids sat huddled together. Dink was shivering.

"Guys, how will we get out of here?" Ruth Rose asked into the darkness. "I didn't see a ladder when we were here this morning."

"I have no idea," Josh said.

Dink thought he heard something. He strained his ears, keeping his eyes locked on the opening.

They all heard the next sound, footsteps coming down the stairs from the top deck.

A head in silhouette appeared over the edge.

Dink shoved himself as close to the wall behind him as he could.

"I know you're down there," a hoarse voice said, floating into the hold. "And there's only one way out. I'm kneeling on the rope ladder."

Dink didn't recognize the voice.

"Do exactly as I say, and I'll drop the ladder for you," the voice went on. "I'm going to lower a basket. Put the jewels in it, and the next thing I send down will be the ladder."

The voice paused. Dink could tell

that Josh and Ruth Rose were trembling.

"If I don't get the jewels, you'll stay here all night, maybe longer," the voice said. "Pretty soon the rats will discover you, and—"

"We'll do it!" Ruth Rose suddenly cried out. "I have the leather bag and the jewels. It's a necklace. You can have it— just promise you'll let us out!"

Dink had never heard Ruth Rose sound so frightened. He could feel her pulling something from her sweatshirt pouch. She dropped it in the darkness, and he heard her fingers scrabbling to find it again.

A basket appeared over their heads, tied to the end of a rope.

It landed on the mattress pile.

"Do it now," the voice said. "Or you'll miss your Thanksgiving dinner!"

Ruth Rose crawled over to the basket. "Okay, the necklace is in the basket.

Now you have to let us out!" Ruth Rose yelled toward the opening.

The kids watched the basket rise and disappear.

Ruth Rose came back and huddled on the mattress. "Sorry, guys," she said. "I had to give it to her or we'd never get out of here!"

They heard laughter from above. A moment later, the rope ladder flew down. It smacked loudly on a mattress.

Dink heard something else land. Whatever it was bounced from the mattress to the wood deck. Dink hoped it wasn't the rat looking for more of Josh's M&M's.

The kids stared at the rope ladder. No one moved. Dink felt sick at the thought that the old woman was still up there, watching for them to climb out of the hold.

They waited in the dark.

"Should we go?" Ruth Rose asked.

"Yeah, I'm outta here!" Josh said. "She must've taken off by now."

Dink held the bottom rung of the rope ladder as Josh and then Ruth Rose climbed up. Dink went up last, the ladder swinging as he climbed.

They pulled the ladder up and piled it next to the opening. Then they tugged the grate back into place.

"It must be after six by now," Dink said as the kids scrambled off the *Mayflower II*. "My mom is going to freak."

They climbed the fence and ran toward the hotel for the second time that night. Now that the snow had almost stopped, a bright moon shone from between the clouds. Dink would have enjoyed the scene if he hadn't been so scared.

This time the woman waiting inside

GOVERNOR
BRADFORD
HOTEL

the hotel lobby was Dink's mother.

She ran toward the kids as they burst into the lobby, out of breath and dirty from being in the hold.

"Donald David Duncan, where have you been?" his mother asked. Her voice shook with worry. "I've been looking all over town for you. Do you remember we agreed on five o'clock?" She checked her watch. "It's well after six!"

Dink felt his face turn red. He didn't know where to start with his story. "I'm

sorry, Mom," he finally said. "Could we go upstairs? I'm really tired and hungry. We have a lot to tell you!"

Dink's mother wrinkled her nose, then she grinned. "You three smell!" she said. "Hot showers first, then I'll call down for some food."

CHAPTER 7

Wearing clean jeans and a sweater, Dink sat with Josh and Ruth Rose on the sofa. Ruth Rose had changed into her pajamas, yellow from top to bottom. Josh was wearing fresh sweats. All three still had damp hair.

While Dink was showering, his mother had sent out for pizza. Dink grabbed a slice and began eating. He started to talk and nearly choked.

"Finish eating," his mother said. "Now that my heart is beating at its normal rate, I can wait a few more minutes to hear your story."

Ten minutes later, after the pizza box had been emptied and cleared, the kids told their story.

"We went to see the *Mayflower II*," Dink said. "A woman on the boat told us about some jewels that got stolen from a passenger."

"Do you mean a jewelry theft on the actual *Mayflower*?" his mother asked. "In 1620?"

Dink nodded.

"That's when the whole story really started," Josh put in. "A crew member on the *Mayflower* stole the jewels, then he disappeared and they were never found!"

Dink, Josh, and Ruth Rose took turns describing everything that had happened to them that day.

Dink's mother's eyes got wide when they told her how they dug up the decaying leather bag and the necklace.

But her face turned white when they described how they got trapped in the *Mayflower II* hold and what happened next.

"So Ruth Rose had to give the jewels to the old woman who'd been following us," Josh said. "After she got the jewels, she threw down the rope ladder so we could get out."

"And then we ran back here," Dink said. "So that's why we were late, Mom."

"That is the most amazing story I've ever heard!" Dink's mother said.

"Actually, we left part of the story out," Ruth Rose said. She glanced at Dink and Josh. "There's something even you guys don't know."

Ruth Rose went across the hall to her bedroom and came back holding a sock. She reached a hand into the sock. "I didn't give the old woman the

Mayflower necklace," she told them. "I switched it with that cheap toy one I got out of the machine this morning."

She pulled her hand out of the sock. She was holding the necklace they'd dug up in Rock Park.

Josh leaped up and gave Ruth Rose a bear hug. "You are awesome!" he cried. "How'd you ever pull it off?"

"I did it when we were hiding down in the hold," Ruth Rose said. "I took my necklace off and rubbed it around in that slimy stuff on the floor so it would look like it had been in the ground."

"May I see it?" Dink's mother asked.

Ruth Rose carefully handed her the necklace.

"These stones look like sapphires," Dink's mother said. "I'm sure this neck-lace is very valuable."

"The passenger who brought them onto the *Mayflower* was Emma Browne,"

Ruth Rose said. "Maybe we can go online and see if she has any relatives, then we can return the necklace."

Dink's mother nodded. "That's a lovely idea," she said. "But for tonight, this is going in the hotel safe. Tomorrow morning I'll call the local police. They may know the old woman who tried to rob you."

That night, Dink dreamed that he was being chased through a blizzard. In his dream, dark, grasping fingers were reaching for him out of the snow. The faster he ran, the more hands appeared, until there were hundreds of fingers, all trying to grab him.

Dink bolted upright, with the bed-covers twisted around his trembling legs. When he realized he'd been dreaming, he lay back down. He looked over at the next bed. Josh was sound asleep.

Dink thought he knew why he'd had that nightmare. The hands belonged to the old woman who'd followed them. Ruth Rose had given her the wrong necklace. And now in Dink's dream, she was coming back for the right one.

Dink felt certain that this dream would come true. Somehow, the woman would come after Dink, Josh, and Ruth Rose again. And this time, she wouldn't be fooled. This thought kept him awake for hours.

Dink's mom and the kids were finishing breakfast in the hotel dining room when two police officers appeared. They all moved into the lobby, and the kids told their story again.

Dink was asked to describe the woman, and he did. The baggy clothing and scraggly hair, the fingerless gloves, the cheek mole.

"Where did you first notice her?" one officer asked.

"On the ferryboat," Dink said. "Then everywhere we went, she seemed to be there, too."

"And as far as you know, you'd never seen her before?"

Dink shook his head. "But she did look familiar," he said. "I mean, there was something about her that reminded me of someone else. I just can't figure out who."

"Did she ever speak to you?"

Dink looked at Josh and Ruth Rose. "Just when we were in the *Mayflower II* hold," he said. "Her voice sounded hoarse, kind of whispery."

"Could you get her fingerprints off that basket she lowered to us?" Josh asked.

"We can try," one of the officers said. "Is it still aboard the *Mayflower II*?"

Josh nodded. "It was there when we left," he said.

"These jewels, where are they now?" the other officer asked.

"In the hotel safe," Dink's mother said. "I called my attorney this morning. He told me they should remain there until we figure out who the rightful owner is."

After a few more questions, the officers left. They said they'd put the word out to watch for this woman.

"I have to go to the restaurant," Dink's mother told the kids. "Altogether there will be twelve of us for dinner tomorrow, and I want to talk to the chef. Then I have to do a few more errands. I shouldn't be too long."

Dink's mom looked him in the eyes. "Please stay around town. No more ferryboat rides to who knows where!" she said firmly.

When they were alone, Dink told Josh and Ruth Rose about his dream. "I think that woman will come back looking for the real necklace," he said.

"Well, I don't know about you guys," Josh said, "but I don't feel like waiting for her to come and find us. I say we go find her first!"

"We don't know who she is," Ruth Rose reminded them.

"I've been thinking about her," Dink went on. "And now I don't think she really is old. There was something weird about her hair, and that mole on her face looked fake. And she managed to get places faster than we did. I think she disguised herself so we'd think she was old."

"Then who is she?" asked Ruth Rose.

"I don't know," Dink said, "but she must know we could recognize her without the disguise."

"We talked to two women yesterday," Josh said, holding up two fingers.
"One was working on the *Mayflower,* and
she was dressed like a Pilgrim. But she
didn't know we were going to Provincetown on the ferry, so she couldn't have
followed us."

"And the other woman was in the
museum," Ruth Rose said.

Josh nodded. "She gets my vote. I
borrowed the magnifying glass from her,
and she could've overheard us when we
were talking about the jewels."

"We should go talk to her," Dink
said. "If she doesn't know we suspect
her, she might drop a clue!"

The kids trekked up the street to the
museum. When they walked through
the door, Clint came right over to see
them.

"Back so soon?" he asked. "How are
things at the Governor Bradford Hotel?"

"Fine thanks," Ruth Rose said. "Our families are coming tomorrow." She glanced around but didn't see the woman they were looking for.

"That woman who was working with you yesterday was real nice," Josh said. "We wanted to thank her. Is she around?"

"She comes in at noon to relieve me," Clint said. He was slapping his pockets, as if looking for something. "Rats, I can't find my mints." He let out a little laugh. "Clint needs a mint!"

A family of tourists came through the door, and Clint went over to greet them.

Dink watched Clint walk away. He listened as Clint talked about the museum exhibits and took their money. And suddenly Dink knew the truth. He grabbed Josh and Ruth Rose, tugging them into another room.

"What's going on?" Josh asked.

"Dink, you look sick," Ruth Rose said. "What's wrong?"

Dink drew his two friends into a huddle. "The old woman is Clint!" he said.

CHAPTER 8

Josh shook his head. "Clint is a woman?" he asked.

"No, but he was dressed as one when he followed us yesterday," Dink said. "Clint knew about the jewels, he knew we suspected that drawing was a map, and he knew we were headed for Provincetown on the ferry!"

"So he disguised himself as an old woman?" Ruth Rose asked.

Dink nodded. "Yes, so we wouldn't know it was him following us."

"What tipped you off?" Josh asked.

"He talked about the Governor

Bradford Hotel a minute ago," Dink answered. "The woman who was here yesterday didn't know we were staying there. Only Clint knew, because we told him!"

"So that was Clint waiting for us last night in the lobby?" Josh asked.

Dink nodded. "He knew we'd go there when we got off the ferry," he said. "So he went there hoping to steal the necklace from us."

"He told us he's an actor, so he could have gotten that costume pretty easily," Ruth Rose said.

"Another thing," Dink went on. "He was missing his mints, right? Well, I'll bet you a million dollars I know where he lost them."

Josh and Ruth Rose just stared at Dink.

"Clint's mints are on the deck of the hold, next to that pile of mattresses,"

Dink said. "I heard something fall last night when he threw down the rope ladder."

Josh peeked around the corner. "He's still talking to those people," he said. "What do we do now?"

"We call those cops back," Dink said. "We'll tell them I can prove Clint tried to steal the necklace."

"Prove it how?" Josh asked. "How do we prove he put on a dress and followed us? How do we prove he was the one who got Ruth Rose's fake necklace last night? Dink, it'll be his word against ours."

"But Clint's fingerprints will be on that basket he lowered down to us!" Ruth Rose said.

"Right, and on his mints container," Dink added.

"Okay, his prints might be on those things," Josh said. "But the cops won't arrest him just because we say we think he dressed like an old woman and followed us. We need to prove he was really trying to steal the necklace."

"I think I know how we can do that," Ruth Rose said. "We'll trick him into trying to rob the necklace from my bedroom."

"It's not in your bedroom anymore," Dink said. "My mom put it in the hotel safe, remember?"

Ruth Rose grinned. "Yeah, we know that, but Clint doesn't!"

Dink shook his head. "Ruth Rose, Clint could be dangerous," he said. "We have to tell the cops about your plan."

"Okay, but let me put out the bait first," Ruth Rose said. "Then the cops can spring the trap!"

The kids walked back into the museum's main room. They pretended to be looking at a painting while Clint finished up with the other people.

A few minutes later, Clint joined them. "So, what brings you back to the museum?" he asked.

Ruth Rose looked at Dink and Josh. "Should I tell Clint what we found yesterday?" she asked.

Dink didn't know what to say, so he nodded.

Ruth Rose turned back to Clint. Keeping her voice low, she whispered, "We found the *Mayflower* jewels!"

Clint just stood there blinking.

Then Ruth Rose told him how they went to Provincetown on the ferry and found the jewels. She also told Clint about the old woman who had made them give her the jewels.

Ruth Rose laughed. "But I gave her a fake necklace!" she said, making her eyes big. "I still have the real one!"

"You . . . you do?" Clint asked.

Ruth Rose nodded smugly. "Yep. But not on me. I have this teddy bear, the kind that has a zippered compartment for your pajamas. I hid the necklace inside it!" she said. "When that old woman figures out we gave her a worthless necklace, she'll come looking for the real one. But even if she searches all over room 202, she'll never find it!"

Clint licked his lips.

Ruth Rose lowered her voice. "And we're gonna sell it! Dink's mom called some jeweler, and he's coming at one o'clock to buy the necklace!"

Dink stared at Ruth Rose. This plan of hers was getting complicated!

"Yeah," Josh said. "This jeweler guy told us the necklace is worth a million dollars. It's all sapphires, man!"

Ruth Rose looked at Dink and Josh. "You guys ready?"

Dink nodded. He was afraid to

speak. His heart was beating so fast he
was sure Clint could hear it if he opened
his mouth!

"We're taking a taxi over to Plimoth Plantation," Ruth Rose said. "We want to see how the Pilgrims lived after they got here."

"You'll enjoy that place," Clint said. "Um, what time does your taxi come?"

Dink looked at his watch. "Yikes, right now!" he said.

The kids said good-bye to Clint, then raced back to their hotel.

They ran up the stairs to room 202, the room Ruth Rose would share with her brother, Nate.

"Old Clint took the bait!" Josh crowed.

"Do you really think he'll come?" Dink asked when they were locked behind Ruth Rose's door.

"Yep," Ruth Rose said. She placed her teddy bear in the middle of her bed. "Now we can call the cops."

CHAPTER 9

The kids waited in room 203, right across the hall from 202. They took turns peeking out the little peephole.

"Poor old Clint is sure gonna be surprised when he finds out there's nothing but jammies inside your bear, Ruth Rose," Josh said.

"And three cops in the closet," Ruth Rose added.

Dink kept his eye on the peephole.

Josh picked up a magazine and began reading.

Ruth Rose did a crossword puzzle.

Suddenly Dink yelled, "Oh no!"

Josh bolted up on the bed, and Ruth Rose froze.

"Is it Clint?" Josh asked.

"No, it's them!" Dink said, throwing open the door.

Standing in the hallway surrounded by luggage were Dink's parents and Josh's and Ruth Rose's families.

"Look who I found in the lobby!" Dink's mom said. His father came to give Dink a hug, but Dink dragged him into room 203.

"Everybody, you have to get in here now!" Dink hissed. "And be quiet!"

"What do you mean?" Ruth Rose's dad asked. "What's going on?"

"Mom and Dad, please. Everyone

just come in, okay?" Ruth Rose said. "We'll explain!"

"Okay, but this is pretty mysterious," Ruth Rose's mother muttered.

The six adults and three little kids all lugged their stuff into room 203. Dink closed the door and locked it.

"Okay, now everyone has to be *real* quiet!" Dink said.

"Especially you two," Josh told his twin brothers, Brian and Bradley.

"We're always quiet!" Brian yelled.

"But I'm the quietest!" Bradley yelled.

"Guys, this is serious!" Dink said. "So if everyone could just please sit down somewhere, Josh, Ruth Rose, and I will tell you what's going on."

. . .

When Dink, Josh, and Ruth Rose had finished telling the story, their families stared at them. No one said a word. Even the twins and Nate sat with their mouths open.

"If I have this right, we're waiting for this thief to show up and burgle Ruth Rose's room," Dink's mother finally said. "Why wasn't I informed of this scheme?"

Dink gulped. "We didn't really think of it till after you left," he said. "But don't worry, the cops are across the hall."

"This is the most exciting Thanksgiving I've ever had!" said Ruth Rose's brother, Nate. "Cops and robbers is a lot more fun than eating turkey!"

Dink's father glanced at his watch. "It's after twelve. When is this burglary supposed to happen?" he asked.

Suddenly they all heard a loud voice

yell, "FREEZE, POLICE!"

"It's Clint!" Dink cried. "They got him!"

Josh ran for the door.

"You freeze, too, young man," Josh's father said. "No one goes into the hall until the police say it's safe." He turned around and put his eye to the peephole.

After three or four long minutes, they all heard a light knock on the door. Josh's father opened it. Three police officers stood there surrounding Clint. He was in handcuffs.

"Mission accomplished," the female officer said. She handed the teddy bear to Ruth Rose.

203

Clint looked at Dink, Josh, and Ruth Rose. "I'm really sorry," he mumbled.

The kids didn't say anything. Ruth Rose hugged her teddy bear as the officers led Clint down the long hallway toward the elevators.

The three families unpacked. There was a lot of laughter and confusion as the adults decided who would sleep where.

Dink's father kept muttering to Dink. "I let you out of my sight for two days, and suddenly there are trapdoors and burglars!" he said. "Why can't you kids just watch TV like normal kids?"

Dink laughed. "Because you keep telling me not to watch TV," he said, then added slyly, "and I always do what you tell me to do."

This got a laugh from Dink's mom.

Finally, everyone was settled and unpacked. They all decided to spend the afternoon at Plimoth Plantation, a reconstruction of the original Plymouth Colony. It was a short drive from the hotel.

After they parked, the three families walked into the village. They saw small wooden homes with thatched roofs. Men, women, and children worked and played. They were all dressed the way people from England would have dressed in the early 1600s.

The group split up and agreed to meet back at the entrance in one hour. Dink, Josh, and Ruth Rose wandered along the gravel paths. They peeked inside homes where women cooked, sewed, or did other chores. They watched men in a field chopping wood.

"This is how the village looked in 1627," Ruth Rose read from her guidebook. "They even shared a cow so everyone could have milk."

Josh stopped in front of a small building. It had only one small window, with stout wooden bars. A man in dark clothing was standing in the doorway.

"This is the village jail," he explained to the kids. "Wrongdoers had to spend time in here."

"What kind of crimes did they commit?" Josh asked.

"Being lazy, not sharing, not attending church," the man said. "If you stole a pig or a hen, that would get you in here, too."

"I wonder if Clint will go to jail," Ruth Rose said as they kept walking. "I mean, he didn't really steal anything."

"He would have if we didn't stop him," Dink said.

Josh nudged Ruth Rose. "Don't forget that Clint broke into your room," he said. "And he threatened to let the rats get us!"

Ruth Rose shuddered. "Yeah, you're right," she said.

The kids kept wandering among the homes. They saw men and women working in gardens and adding thatch to the roofs of buildings. They looked inside a small room where a man was teaching children to learn their letters and numbers. Each child held a small slate and chalk.

"I've been thinking about the necklace we found," Ruth Rose said. "I think we should donate it to the Pilgrim Hall Museum."

"Excellent," Dink said. "That way everyone who visits would get to see Emma Browne's jewelry."

"Cool idea, Ruth Rose," Josh agreed. "Remember that pamphlet about the 'Muddlesome *Mayflower* Mystery'? Well, if we give the necklace to the museum, people can see the necklace and know the mystery has been solved."

CHAPTER 10

The next day, the twelve family members walked to a restaurant called the Pilgrim's Pantry. The sun was out, and last night's snow had melted.

Inside, they were greeted by a woman dressed in a white shirt, a long dark apron, and a tight-fitting white bonnet. She led them to a large round table. Turkey-shaped name cards had been set at each place, and everyone found his or her seat easily.

Ruth Rose sat between Dink and Josh. She was wearing the fake necklace. In honor of the holiday, she had chosen pumpkin orange as her color for the day.

"The police called and told us you were right about the mints, Dink," his father said. "They were in the *Mayflower II* hold, on the deck. And they were able to get Clint's fingerprints off them."

"So Clint's mints had prints," Josh joked, waggling his eyebrows.

"That was a great idea you kids had to give the necklace to the museum," Josh's father said. "I'm sure they'll love to have it." He winked at the kids. "And of course, they'd need a picture of you three ace detectives."

"Awesome!" Josh said. "I'm going to be in a museum!"

A waiter approached their table. He wore black breeches, a white ruffled shirt, and clunky black shoes. "Good afternoon," he said. "Today we're serving from our regular menu, or you can

order our First Thanksgiving Special—
four courses of foods the Pilgrims would
really have eaten in 1621."

"That's what I want," Dink said.

"Did the Pilgrims have pumpkin pie
with whipped cream?" Josh asked.

The waiter smiled. "The early settlers had pumpkins but no sugar, so they
probably didn't make pies," he said.
"But you can order your dessert from
our regular menu."

"Thank goodness!" Josh said. "You
saved me!"

Everyone laughed.

"They had turkeys, though, right?"
Nate asked the waiter.

"Yes, wild turkeys were plentiful,"
the man said. "They also ate clams,
many kinds of fish, venison, and any
wild bird they could find. You folks take
your time deciding, and I'll stop back in
a few minutes."

"Indians came to Plymouth to eat with the settlers, right?" Dink asked.

"Yes, the Wampanoag were here," his father said. "They became friendly with the Pilgrims."

"My guidebook says almost a hundred Wampanoag people showed up to eat with the Pilgrims after their first harvest," Ruth Rose said.

Just then the waiter came back to take their order. The three little kids ordered from the regular menu. Dink, Josh, Ruth Rose, and their parents all decided to try the First Thanksgiving Special.

The waiter returned. He carried a tray holding small bowls and a covered soup tureen. Dink smelled something delicious. His mouth began to water.

"Our first course is eel stew," the man said. "May I serve you?"

Josh's face turned white. "Um, eels?

You mean those slimy things that look like snakes?" he asked the waiter.

The waiter nodded.

"May I change to the regular menu?" Josh asked.

DID YOU FIND THE
SECRET MESSAGE
HIDDEN IN THIS BOOK?

If you *don't* want
to know the answer,
don't look at the bottom
of this page!

HAVE YOU READ ALL THE BOOKS IN THE

A to Z Mysteries®

SERIES?

Help Dink, Josh, and Ruth Rose . . .

...solve
mysteries
from A to Z!

Collect clues with
Dink, Josh, and Ruth Rose
in their next exciting
adventure

WHITE HOUSE WHITE-OUT

The kids were knocked off balance as the van suddenly backed up. Then there was a sharp turn, and they fell again as the van lurched forward.

"Where are we going?" Ruth Rose whispered in the dark.

"We don't have to whisper. The driver can't hear us," Dink said. The wall that separated them from the front cab would absorb all sounds from the back.

"Guys, I think we're being kidnapped!" Josh said.

A TO Z MYSTERIES® fans, check out Ron Roy's other great mystery series!

Capital Mysteries

#1: Who Cloned the President?
#2: Kidnapped at the Capital
#3: The Skeleton in the Smithsonian
#4: A Spy in the White House
#5: Who Broke Lincoln's Thumb?
#6: Fireworks at the FBI
#7: Trouble at the Treasury
#8: Mystery at the Washington Monument
#9: A Thief at the National Zoo
#10: The Election-Day Disaster
#11: The Secret at Jefferson's Mansion
#12: The Ghost at Camp David
#13: Trapped on the D.C. Train!
#14: Turkey Trouble on the National Mall

January Joker
February Friend
March Mischief
April Adventure
May Magic
June Jam
July Jitters
August Acrobat
September Sneakers
October Ogre
November Night
December Dog
New Year's Eve Thieves

If you like **A TO Z MYSTERIES**®,
take a swing at

BALLPARK® Mysteries

#1: The Fenway Foul-Up
#2: The Pinstripe Ghost
#3: The L.A. Dodger
#4: The Astro Outlaw
#5: The All-Star Joker
#6: The Wrigley Riddle
#7: The San Francisco Splash
#8: The Missing Marlin
#9: The Philly Fake
#10: The Rookie Blue Jay
#11: The Tiger Troubles

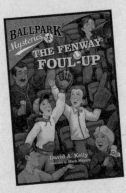